Bear COUNTS

Karma Wilson

Illustrations by
Jane Chapman

SCHOLASTIC INC.

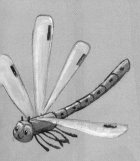

Mouse and Bear share breakfast,
basking in the morning sun.
Bear looks up and points,
and the bear
counts . . .

one!

One sun floating high.
One giant dragonfly.

One robin on her nest.
Only ONE berry left!

Numbers, numbers everywhere.
Can you count along with Bear?

Mouse and Bear see Hare,
and Hare calls out, "Howdy do?"
He is holding yummy fruit,
and the bear

counts . . .

two!

Two paws which hold a treat.
Two apples crisp and sweet!

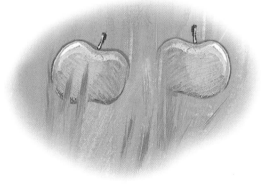

Two stumps for perfect chairs.
Two friends who love to share.

Numbers, numbers everywhere.
Can you count along with Bear?

1,2!

Bear hears funny sounds
coming from an aspen tree.
It is Raven, Owl, and Wren,
and the bear

counts . . .

three!

Three chums who chitter-chat.
Three funny muskrats.

Three clouds above the trees.

Three bumbling bumblebees.

Numbers, numbers everywhere.
Can you count along with Bear?

1,2,3!

Bear cries, "Look, it's Badger,
Mole, and Gopher by the shore!
Badger has his fishin' pole."
And the bear
counts . . .

four!

Four fish splish 'n' splash.

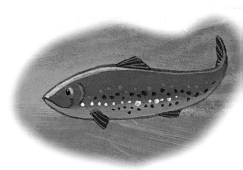

Four geese waddle past.

Four turtles on a log.

Four croaking, hopping frogs!

Numbers, numbers everywhere.
Can you count along with Bear?

1,2,3,4!

Mouse squeaks, "Let's go swimming!"
And in the pond they dive.
The friends float in the pond.
And the bear
counts . . .

five!

Five ducks in the water.

Five lively river otters.

Five lovely lily pads.

Five pinching crawdads.

Numbers, numbers everywhere.
Now YOU can count, just like BEAR!

1!

2!

3!

One, two, three gorgeous kids! Can you count with Karma?
To Sarah, Nathan, David Brian, Atticus Daniel,
and Louisa Belle. All my love!
—K. W.

To Dylan, Jacob, and Bump
—J. C.

ISBN 978-0-545-91217-4

Text copyright © 2015 by Karma Wilson. Illustrations copyright © 2015 by Jane Chapman. All rights reserved. Published by Scholastic Inc., 557 Broadway, New York, NY 10012, by arrangement with Margaret K. McElderry Books, an imprint of Simon & Schuster Children's Publishing Division. SCHOLASTIC and associated logos are trademarks and/or registered trademarks of Scholastic Inc.

12 11 10 9   19 20 21

Printed in the U.S.A.   40

First Scholastic paperback printing, September 2016

Book design by Lauren Rille
The text for this book is set in Adobe Caslon.
The illustrations for this book are rendered in acrylic paint.